THE WHOLE ALPHABET IS TOTALLY EMBARRASSED

michelle thornhill

 For M-Y-L-A

First Printing 2017
Second Printing 2019
Paperback Edition 2020

ISBN 978-1-9992620-3-7

Readosaurus Press

A accidentally asked for anchovies and made an awful aroma in his apartment.

B burped out a bubble in front of the boss.

C got caught crunching
cinnamon candies in church.

D's Dad did a disco dance.
It was a disaster.

E is easily embarrassed every
time he eats eleven eggs.

**F farted so forcefully
he frightened a fish.**

G gets all **g**oo**g**ly-eyed and **g**i**gg**ly when he talks to **g**irls.

H hiccuped so horribly that someone hurled a hamburger at his head.

I had the irrational idea to sell
ice cream on the Internet.

J told a joke nobody enjoyed.

K tried to kiss a kangaroo.
She got kicked.

L led a lion into the library
and he was loud.

M made a mistake and called
the mailman "Mommy."

N had a **nose nugget.**
His **Nana noticed.**

O overflowed the only
toilet in the office.

P peed his pants at a party.

Q quacked at the queen.

R is about to realize that those random raisins aren't really raisins.

S got sprayed by seven smelly skunks.

T was terrified by a toy Tyrannosaurus and tumbled into the toilet.

U has ugly, uncomfortable underwear.

V vomited on vacation.

W walked on a whoopee cushion at her wedding.

X ran into her ex-boyfriend and couldn't explain the extra large box of ex-lax.

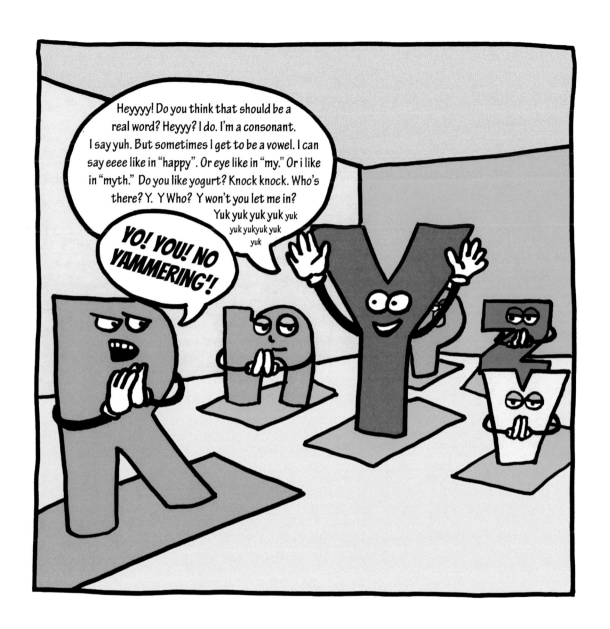

Y got yelled at in yoga for yakking.

Z rode a **z**ip-line into the end **z**one
of a **z**ebra at the **z**oo.

Made in the USA
Middletown, DE
13 August 2021